The Jungle Book

retold by Diane Stortz

Fairy Tale Classics

LANDOLL
Ashland, Ohio 44805

On a warm, summer evening deep in the jungle in India, Mother and Father Wolf and their four cubs awoke from a nap in their cave.

Mother Wolf pricked up her ears. "Listen!" she said. "Something is coming up the hill."

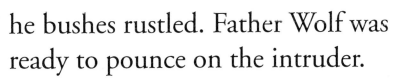

he bushes rustled. Father Wolf was ready to pounce on the intruder. Suddenly, he relaxed. "Look!" he said. "It is a man cub."

Soft and smooth and barely big enough to walk, the little boy looked up at Father Wolf and laughed. Father Wolf picked him up gently and carried him inside.

"How little! How sweet and how brave!" said Mother Wolf softly. The little man cub pushed his way between the wolf cubs to get warm.

Was there ever a wolf mother with a man cub among her children?" asked Mother Wolf.

"I have heard of such things," said Father Wolf. "But never before among the wolves of our pack."

Suddenly the wolves heard a low growl. It was Shere Khan, the tiger, and he was too big to fit through the mouth of the cave. "Give me the man cub. He is mine," said the tiger. But the wolves would not turn over the man cub, and Shere Khan angrily went away. Mother Wolf named the man cub Mowgli.

The law of the jungle said that all wolf cubs old enough to stand must be brought to the pack council, held at the full moon, to be identified. Father Wolf took Mowgli and his own four wolf cubs to the meeting of the pack at Council Rock. Mowgli and the cubs played with pebbles that shone in the moonlight while the other wolves sat around them in a circle.

With the wolves at this meeting was Baloo, the sleepy old brown bear who ate only nuts and roots and honey. Baloo was the teacher of all the wolf cubs. "Let the man cub run with the pack," said Baloo. "I will teach him the ways of the jungle."

In the distance, behind Council Rock, the growls of Shere Khan could be heard. Then Bagheera, the inky black panther, spoke. "Accept the man cub," Bagheera said. "I will be his guardian." The wolves all listened to both Baloo and Bagheera, and decided that Father and Mother Wolf should keep the man cub to raise as their own son.

he next ten years were wonderful years for Mowgli. He called the wolves and the other jungle animals his brothers. He played games with the wolf cubs during the day and slept soundly next to them at night. He ate coconuts, and bananas, and sweet pawpaws from the trees of the jungle, and drank from the clear jungle streams. Father Wolf, Baloo, and Bagheera taught Mowgli the ways of the jungle, and when he was old enough, he met at Council Rock with the rest of the pack.

ne day, Bagheera had a long talk with Mowgli. "You must be ready," Bagheera said. "Someday Shere Khan will come after you. The only way you can be safe, and keep the jungle safe from Shere Khan, is to return to the man village." This news made Mowgli very sad. But because he loved Bagheera and the other jungle animals, he obeyed.

"I will go from the jungle to my own people," Mowgli said. He went to the cave where he had been raised and said good-bye to Father and Mother Wolf, and to his wolf brothers. They promised to visit him at the edge of the farmlands near the man village. And Mowgli promised that someday he would return to the jungle.

hen Mowgli reached the man village, a rich woman named Messua gave him a long drink of milk and some bread. Messua and her husband decided that Mowgli should stay with them. "I might as well," Mowgli said to himself. "At least until I have learned man's language." In the jungle, Mowgli had learned to imitate the sounds of many of the animals, and before dark he had learned the names of many of the things in the house.

Soon Mowgli could speak man's language well. He learned to wear clothes, to count money, to farm, and to herd buffalo. But, his wolf brothers still met him at the edge of the farmlands to run and play and tell him the news of the jungle.

One day, Gray Brother brought news that Shere Khan was once more looking for Mowgli, just as Bagheera had warned. "He plans to wait for you at the village gate this evening," said Gray Brother.

But before the tiger could find Mowgli, Mowgli surprised the tiger. Riding on the back of a buffalo, and with help from Gray Brother, Mowgli herded all the buffalo toward the village gate. The tiger was so surprised and frightened that he ran away without a fight.

 owgli took the buffalo back to the man village. Then he said good-bye to the family that had taken him in, and returned to the jungle...his true home. What a happy meeting there was at Council Rock that night! And for the rest of his life, Mowgli lived in the jungle with Baloo and Bagheera and Gray Wolf and the other wolves for company.